Eugene Pickering

Henry James

Pharos Books

ISBN: 978-93-58044-45-4
eISBN: 978-93-58044-47-8

©Publisher

Publisher: Pharos Books (P) Ltd.
Plot No.-63, 1st Floor, Main Mother Dairy Road
Pandav Nagar, East Delhi-110092
Phone: 011-40395855, +4049916623
WhatsApp: +91 9319228272
E-mail: sales@pharosbooks.in
Website: www.pharosbooks.in
First Edition: 2025

Printed By: Sushma Book Binding House, Okhla
Industrial Area, Phase II, New Delhi-110020

EUGENE PICKERING
Henry James

CONTENTS

EUGENE PICKERING

CHAPTER I

It was at Homburg, several years ago, before the gaming had been suppressed. The evening was very warm, and all the world was gathered on the terrace of the Kursaal and the esplanade below it to listen to the excellent orchestra; or half the world, rather, for the crowd was equally dense in the gaming-rooms around the tables. Everywhere the crowd was great. The night was perfect, the season was at its height, the open windows of the Kursaal sent long shafts of unnatural light into the dusky woods, and now and then, in the intervals of the music, one might almost hear the clink of the napoleons and the metallic call of the croupiers rise above the watching silence of the saloons. I had been strolling with a friend, and we at last prepared to sit down. Chairs, however, were scarce. I had captured one, but it seemed no easy matter to find a mate for it. I was on the point of giving up in despair, and proposing an adjournment to the silken ottomans of the Kursaal, when I observed a young man lounging back on one of the objects of my quest, with his feet supported on the rounds of another. This was more than his share of luxury, and I promptly approached him. He evidently belonged to the race which has the credit of knowing best, at home and abroad, how to make itself comfortable; but something in his appearance suggested that his present attitude was the result of inadvertence rather than of egotism. He was staring at the conductor of the orchestra and listening intently to the music. His hands were locked round his long legs, and his mouth was half open, with rather a foolish air. "There are so few chairs," I said, "that I must beg you to surrender this second one." He started, stared, blushed, pushed the chair away with awkward alacrity, and murmured something about not having noticed that he had it.

"What an odd-looking youth!" said my companion, who had watched me, as I seated myself beside her.

"Yes, he is odd-looking; but what is odder still is that I have seen him before, that his face is familiar to me, and yet that I can't place him." The orchestra was playing the Prayer from Der Freischütz, but Weber's lovely music only deepened the blank of memory. Who the deuce was he? where, when, how, had I known him? It seemed extraordinary that a face should be at once so familiar and so strange. We had our backs turned to him, so that I could not look at him again. When the music ceased we left our places, and I went to consign my friend to her mamma on the terrace. In passing, I saw that my young man had departed; I concluded that he only strikingly resembled some one I knew. But who in the world was it he resembled? The ladies went off to their lodgings, which were near by, and I turned into the gaming-rooms and hovered about the circle at roulette. Gradually I filtered through to the inner edge, near the table, and, looking round, saw my puzzling friend stationed opposite to me. He was watching the game, with his hands in his pockets; but singularly enough, now that I observed him at my leisure, the look of familiarity quite faded from his face. What had made us call his appearance odd was his great length and leanness of limb, his long, white neck, his blue, prominent eyes, and his ingenuous, unconscious absorption in the scene before him. He was not handsome, certainly, but he looked peculiarly amiable and if his overt wonderment savoured a trifle of rurality, it was an agreeable contrast to the hard, inexpressive masks about him. He was the verdant offshoot, I said to myself, of some ancient, rigid stem; he had been brought up in the quietest of homes, and he was having his first glimpse of life. I was curious to see whether he would put anything on the table; he evidently felt the temptation, but he seemed paralysed by chronic embarrassment. He stood gazing at the chinking complexity of losses and gains, shaking his loose gold in his pocket, and every now and then passing his hand nervously over his eyes.

Most of the spectators were too attentive to the play to have many thoughts for each other; but before long I noticed a lady who evidently had an eye for her neighbours as well as for the table. She was seated about half-way between my friend and me, and I presently observed that she was trying to catch his eye. Though at Homburg, as people said, "one could never be sure," I yet doubted whether this lady were one of those whose especial vocation it was to catch a gentleman's eye. She was youthful rather than elderly, and pretty rather than plain; indeed, a few minutes later, when I saw her smile, I thought her wonderfully pretty. She had a charming gray eye and a good deal of yellow hair disposed in picturesque disorder; and though her features were meagre and her complexion faded, she gave one a sense of sentimental, artificial gracefulness. She was dressed in white muslin very much puffed and filled, but a trifle the worse for wear, relieved here and there by a pale blue ribbon. I used to flatter myself on guessing at people's nationality by their faces, and, as a rule, I guessed aright. This faded, crumpled, vaporous beauty, I conceived, was a German—such a German, somehow, as I had seen imagined in literature. Was she not a friend of poets, a correspondent of philosophers, a muse, a priestess of æsthetics—something in the way of a Bettina, a Rahel? My conjectures, however, were speedily merged in wonderment as to what my diffident friend was making of her. She caught his eye at last, and raising an ungloved hand, covered altogether with blue-gemmed rings—turquoises, sapphires, and lapis—she beckoned him to come to her. The gesture was executed with a sort of practised coolness, and accompanied with an appealing smile. He stared a moment, rather blankly, unable to suppose that the invitation was addressed to him; then, as it was immediately repeated with a good deal of intensity, he blushed to the roots of his hair, wavered awkwardly, and at last made his way to the lady's chair. By the time he reached it he was crimson, and wiping his forehead with his pocket-handkerchief. She tilted back, looked up at him with the same smile, laid two fingers on his sleeve, and said something, interrogatively, to which he replied by a shake of the head. She was asking him, evidently, if he had ever played, and he was saying no. Old players have a fancy that when luck has turned her back on them they can put her into good-humour again by having their stakes placed by a novice. Our young man's physiognomy had seemed to his new acquaintance to express the perfection of inexperience, and, like a practical woman, she had determined to make him serve her turn. Unlike most of her neighbours, she had no little pile of gold before her, but she drew from her pocket a double napoleon, put it into his hand, and bade him place it on a number of his own choosing. He was evidently filled with a sort of delightful trouble; he enjoyed the adventure, but he shrank from the hazard. I would have staked the coin on its being his companion's last; for although she still smiled intently as she watched his hesitation, there was anything but indifference in her pale, pretty face. Suddenly, in desperation, he reached over and laid the piece on the table. My attention was diverted at this moment by my having to make way for a lady with a great many flounces, before me, to give up her chair to a rustling friend to whom she had promised it; when I again looked across at the lady in white muslin, she was drawing in a very goodly pile of gold with her little blue-gemmed claw. Good luck and bad, at the Homburg tables, were equally undemonstrative, and this happy adventuress rewarded her young friend for the sacrifice of his innocence with a single, rapid, upward smile. He had innocence enough left, however, to look round the table with a gleeful, conscious laugh, in the midst of which his eyes encountered my own. Then suddenly the familiar look which had vanished from his face flickered up unmistakably; it was the boyish laugh of a boyhood's friend. Stupid fellow that I was, I had been looking at Eugene Pickering!

Though I lingered on for some time longer he failed to recognise me. Recognition, I think, had kindled a smile in my own face; but, less fortunate than he, I suppose my smile had ceased to be boyish. Now that luck had faced about again, his companion played for herself—played and won, hand over hand. At last she seemed disposed to rest on her gains, and proceeded to bury them in the folds of her muslin. Pickering had staked nothing for himself, but as he saw her prepare to withdraw he offered her a double napoleon and begged her to place it. She shook her head with great decision, and seemed to bid him put it up again; but he, still blushing a good deal, pressed her with awkward ardour, and she at last took it from him, looked at him a moment fixedly, and laid it on a number. A moment later the croupier was raking it in. She gave the young man a little nod which seemed to say, "I told you so;" he glanced round the table again and laughed; she left her chair, and he made a way for her through the crowd. Before going home I took a turn on the terrace and looked down on the esplanade. The lamps were out, but the warm starlight vaguely illumined a dozen figures scattered in couples. One of these figures, I thought, was a lady in a white dress.

I had no intention of letting Pickering go without reminding him of our old acquaintance. He had been a very singular boy, and I was curious to see what had become of his singularity. I looked for him the next morning at two or three of the hotels, and at last I discovered his whereabouts. But he was out, the waiter said; he had gone to walk an hour before. I went my way, confident that I should meet him in the evening. It was the rule with the Homburg world to spend its evenings at the Kursaal, and Pickering, apparently, had already discovered a good reason for not being an exception. One of the charms of Homburg is the fact that of a hot day you may walk about for a whole afternoon in unbroken shade. The umbrageous gardens of the Kursaal mingle with the charming Hardtwald, which in turn melts away into the wooded slopes of the Taunus Mountains. To the Hardtwald I bent my steps, and strolled for an hour through mossy glades and the still, perpendicular gloom of the fir-woods. Suddenly, on the grassy margin of a by-path, I came upon a young man stretched at his length in the sun-checkered shade, and kicking his heels towards a patch of blue sky. My step was so noiseless on the turf that, before he saw me, I had time to recognise Pickering again. He looked as if he had been lounging there for some time; his hair was tossed about as if he had been sleeping; on the grass near him, beside his hat and stick, lay a sealed letter. When he perceived me he jerked himself forward, and I stood looking at him without introducing myself—purposely, to give him a chance to recognise me. He put on his glasses, being awkwardly near-sighted, and stared up at me with an air of general trustfulness, but without a sign of knowing me. So at last I introduced myself. Then he jumped up and grasped my hands, and stared and blushed and laughed, and began a dozen random questions, ending with a demand as to how in the world I had known him.

"Why, you are not changed so utterly," I said; "and after all, it's but fifteen years since you used to do my Latin exercises for me."

"Not changed, eh?" he answered, still smiling, and yet speaking with a sort of ingenuous dismay.

Then I remembered that poor Pickering had been, in those Latin days, a victim of juvenile irony. He used to bring a bottle of medicine to school and take a dose in a glass of water before lunch; and every day at two o'clock, half an hour before the rest of us were liberated, an old nurse with bushy eyebrows came and fetched him away in a carriage. His extremely fair complexion, his nurse, and his bottle of medicine, which suggested a vague analogy with the sleeping-potion in the tragedy, caused him to be called Juliet. Certainly Romeo's sweetheart hardly suffered more; she was not, at least, a standing joke in Verona. Remembering these things, I hastened to say to Pickering that I hoped he was still the same good fellow who used to do my Latin for me. "We were capital friends, you know," I went on, "then and afterwards."

"Yes, we were very good friends," he said, "and that makes it the stranger I shouldn't have known you. For you know, as a boy, I never had many friends, nor as a man either. You see," he added, passing his hand over his eyes, "I am rather dazed, rather bewildered at finding myself for the first time—alone." And he jerked back his shoulders nervously, and threw up his head, as if to settle himself in an unwonted position. I wondered whether the old nurse with

                                                    EUGENE PICKERING

the bushy eyebrows had remained attached to his person up to a recent period, and discovered presently that, virtually at least, she had. We had the whole summer day before us, and we sat down on the grass together and overhauled our old memories. It was as if we had stumbled upon an ancient cupboard in some dusky corner, and rummaged out a heap of childish playthings—tin soldiers and torn story-books, jack-knives and Chinese puzzles. This is what we remembered between us.

He had made but a short stay at school—not because he was tormented, for he thought it so fine to be at school at all that he held his tongue at home about the sufferings incurred through the medicine-bottle, but because his father thought he was learning bad manners. This he imparted to me in confidence at the time, and I remember how it increased my oppressive awe of Mr. Pickering, who had appeared to me in glimpses as a sort of high priest of the proprieties. Mr. Pickering was a widower—a fact which seemed to produce in him a sort of preternatural concentration of parental dignity. He was a majestic man, with a hooked nose, a keen dark eye, very large whiskers, and notions of his own as to how a boy— or his boy, at any rate—should be brought up. First and foremost, he was to be a "gentleman"; which seemed to mean, chiefly, that he was always to wear a muffler and gloves, and be sent to bed, after a supper of bread and milk, at eight o'clock. School-life, on experiment, seemed hostile to these observances, and Eugene was taken home again, to be moulded into urbanity beneath the parental eye. A tutor was provided for him, and a single select companion was prescribed. The choice, mysteriously, fell on me, born as I was under quite another star; my parents were appealed to, and I was allowed for a few months to have my lessons with Eugene. The tutor, I think, must have been rather a snob, for Eugene was treated like a prince, while I got all the questions and the raps with the ruler. And yet I remember never being jealous of my happier comrade, and striking up, for the time, one of those friendships of childhood. He had a watch and a pony and a great store of picture-books, but my envy of these luxuries was tempered by a vague compassion which left me free to be generous. I could go out to play alone, I could button my jacket myself, and sit up till I was sleepy. Poor Pickering could never take a step without asking leave, or spend half an hour in the garden without a formal report of it when he came in. My parents, who had no desire to see me inoculated with importunate virtues, sent me back to school at the end of six months. After that I never saw Eugene. His father went to live in the country, to protect the lad's morals, and Eugene faded, in reminiscence, into a pale image of the depressing effects of education. I think I vaguely supposed that he would melt into thin air, and indeed began gradually to doubt of his existence, and to regard him as one of the foolish things one ceased to believe in as one grew older. It seemed natural that I should have no more news of him. Our present meeting was my first assurance that he had really survived all that muffling and coddling.

I observed him now with a good deal of interest, for he was a rare phenomenon—the fruit of a system persistently and uninterruptedly applied. He struck me, in a fashion, as certain young monks I had seen in Italy; he had the same candid, unsophisticated cloister face. His education had been really almost monastic. It had found him evidently a very compliant, yielding subject; his gentle affectionate spirit was not one of those that need to be broken. It had bequeathed him, now that he stood on the threshold of the great world, an extraordinary freshness of impression and alertness of desire, and I confess that, as I looked at him and met his transparent blue eye, I trembled for the unwarned innocence of such a soul. I became aware, gradually, that the world had already wrought a certain work upon him and roused him to a restless, troubled self-consciousness. Everything about him pointed to an experience from which he had been debarred; his whole organism trembled with a dawning sense of unsuspected possibilities of feeling. This appealing tremor was indeed outwardly visible. He kept shifting himself about on the grass, thrusting his hands through his hair, wiping a light perspiration from his forehead, breaking out to say something and rushing off to something else.

　　　　　　　　　　　　　　　　　EUGENE PICKERING

Our sudden meeting had greatly excited him, and I saw that I was likely to profit by a certain overflow of sentimental fermentation. I could do so with a good conscience, for all this trepidation filled me with a great friendliness.

"It's nearly fifteen years, as you say," he began, "since you used to call me 'butter-fingers' for always missing the ball. That's a long time to give an account of, and yet they have been, for me, such eventless, monotonous years, that I could almost tell their history in ten words. You, I suppose, have had all kinds of adventures and travelled over half the world. I remember you had a turn for deeds of daring; I used to think you a little Captain Cook in roundabouts, for climbing the garden fence to get the ball when I had let it fly over. I climbed no fences then or since. You remember my father, I suppose, and the great care he took of me? I lost him some five months ago. From those boyish days up to his death we were always together. I don't think that in fifteen years we spent half a dozen hours apart. We lived in the country, winter and summer, seeing but three or four people. I had a succession of tutors, and a library to browse about in; I assure you I am a tremendous scholar. It was a dull life for a growing boy, and a duller life for a young man grown, but I never knew it. I was perfectly happy." He spoke of his father at some length, and with a respect which I privately declined to emulate. Mr. Pickering had been, to my sense, a frigid egotist, unable to conceive of any larger vocation for his son than to strive to reproduce so irreproachable a model. "I know I have been strangely brought up," said my friend, "and that the result is something grotesque; but my education, piece by piece, in detail, became one of my father's personal habits, as it were. He took a fancy to it at first through his intense affection for my mother and the sort of worship he paid her memory. She died at my birth, and as I grew up, it seems that I bore an extraordinary likeness to her. Besides, my father had a great many theories; he prided himself on his conservative opinions; he thought the usual American *laisser-aller* in education was a very vulgar practice, and that children were not to grow up like dusty thorns by the wayside." "So you see,"

Pickering went on, smiling and blushing, and yet with something of the irony of vain regret, "I am a regular garden plant. I have been watched and watered and pruned, and if there is any virtue in tending I ought to take the prize at a flower show. Some three years ago my father's health broke down, and he was kept very much within doors. So, although I was a man grown, I lived altogether at home. If I was out of his sight for a quarter of an hour he sent some one after me. He had severe attacks of neuralgia, and he used to sit at his window, basking in the sun. He kept an opera-glass at hand, and when I was out in the garden he used to watch me with it. A few days before his death I was twenty-seven years old, and the most innocent youth, I suppose, on the continent. After he died I missed him greatly," Pickering continued, evidently with no intention of making an epigram. "I stayed at home, in a sort of dull stupor. It seemed as if life offered itself to me for the first time, and yet as if I didn't know how to take hold of it."

He uttered all this with a frank eagerness which increased as he talked, and there was a singular contrast between the meagre experience he described and a certain radiant intelligence which I seemed to perceive in his glance and tone. Evidently he was a clever fellow, and his natural faculties were excellent. I imagined he had read a great deal, and recovered, in some degree, in restless intellectual conjecture, the freedom he was condemned to ignore in practice. Opportunity was now offering a meaning to the empty forms with which his imagination was stored, but it appeared to him dimly, through the veil of his personal diffidence.

"I have not sailed round the world, as you suppose," I said, "but I confess I envy you the novelties you are going to behold. Coming to Homburg you have plunged *in medias res.*"

He glanced at me to see if my remark contained an allusion, and hesitated a moment. "Yes, I know it. I came to Bremen in the steamer with a very friendly German, who undertook to initiate me into the glories and mysteries of the Fatherland. At this season, he said, I must begin with Homburg. I landed but a fortnight ago, and here I am." Again he hesitated, as if he were going to add something about the scene at the Kursaal but suddenly, nervously, he took up the letter which was lying beside him, looked hard at the seal with a troubled frown, and then flung it back on the grass with a sigh.

"How long do you expect to be in Europe?" I asked.

"Six months I supposed when I came. But not so long—now!" And he let his eyes wander to the letter again.

"And where shall you go—what shall you do?"

"Everywhere, everything, I should have said yesterday. But now it is different."

I glanced at the letter—interrogatively, and he gravely picked it up and put it into his pocket. We talked for a while longer, but I saw that he had suddenly become preoccupied; that he was apparently weighing an impulse to break some last barrier of reserve. At last he suddenly laid his hand on my arm, looked at me a moment appealingly, and cried, "Upon my word, I should like to tell you everything!"

"Tell me everything, by all means," I answered, smiling. "I desire nothing better than to lie here in the shade and hear everything."

"Ah, but the question is, will you understand it? No matter; you think me a queer fellow already. It's not easy, either, to tell you what I feel—not easy for so queer a fellow as I to tell you in how many ways he is queer!" He got up and walked away a moment, passing his hand over his eyes, then came back rapidly and flung himself on the grass again. "I said just now I always supposed I was happy; it's true; but now that my eyes are open, I see I was only stultified. I was like a poodle-dog that is led about by a blue ribbon, and scoured and combed and fed on slops. It was not life; life is learning to know one's self, and in that sense I have lived more in the past six weeks than in all the years that preceded them. I am filled with this feverish sense of liberation; it keeps rising to my head like the fumes of strong wine. I find I am an active, sentient, intelligent creature, with desires, with passions, with possible convictions—even with what I never dreamed of, a possible will of my own! I find there is a world to know, a life to lead, men and women to form a thousand relations with. It all lies there like a great surging sea, where we must plunge and dive and feel the breeze and breast the waves. I stand shivering here on the brink, staring, longing, wondering, charmed by the smell of the brine and yet afraid of the water. The world beckons and smiles and calls, but a nameless influence from the past, that I can neither wholly obey nor wholly resist, seems to hold me back. I am full of impulses, but, somehow, I am not full of strength. Life seems inspiring at certain moments, but it seems terrible and unsafe; and I ask myself why I should wantonly measure myself with merciless forces, when I have learned so well how to stand aside and let them pass. Why shouldn't I turn my back upon it all and go home to— what awaits me?—to that sightless, soundless country life, and long days spent among old books? But if a man *is* weak, he doesn't want to assent beforehand to his weakness; he wants to taste whatever sweetness there may be in paying for the knowledge. So it is that it comes back—this irresistible impulse to take my plunge—to let myself swing, to go where liberty leads me." He paused a moment, fixing me with his excited eyes, and perhaps perceived in my own an irrepressible smile at his perplexity. "'Swing ahead, in Heaven's name,' you want to say, 'and much good may it do you.' I don't know whether you are laughing at my scruples or at what possibly strikes you as my depravity. I doubt," he went on gravely, "whether I have an inclination toward wrong-doing; if I have, I am sure I shall not prosper in it. I honestly believe I may safely take out a license to amuse myself. But it isn't that I think of, any more than I dream of, playing with suffering. Pleasure and pain are empty words to me; what I long for is knowledge—some other knowledge than comes to us in formal, colourless, impersonal precept. You would understand all this better if you could breathe for an hour the musty in-door atmosphere in which I have always lived. To break a window and let in light and air—I feel as if at last I must *act!*"

                                           EUGENE PICKERING

"Act, by all means, now and always, when you have a chance," I answered. "But don't take things too hard, now or ever. Your long confinement makes you think the world better worth knowing than you are likely to find it. A man with as good a head and heart as yours has a very ample world within himself, and I am no believer in art for art, nor in what's called 'life' for life's sake. Nevertheless, take your plunge, and come and tell me whether you have found the pearl of wisdom." He frowned a little, as if he thought my sympathy a trifle meagre. I shook him by the hand and laughed. "The pearl of wisdom," I cried, "is love; honest love in the most convenient concentration of experience! I advise you to fall in love." He gave me no smile in response, but drew from his pocket the letter of which I have spoken, held it up, and shook it solemnly. "What is it?" I asked.

"It is my sentence!"

"Not of death, I hope!"

"Of marriage."

"With whom?"

"With a person I don't love."

This was serious. I stopped smiling, and begged him to explain.

"It is the singular part of my story," he said at last. "It will remind you of an old-fashioned romance. Such as I sit here, talking in this wild way, and tossing off provocations to destiny, my destiny is settled and sealed. I am engaged, I am given in marriage. It's a bequest of the past—the past I had no hand in! The marriage was arranged by my father, years ago, when I was a boy. The young girl's father was his particular friend; he was also a widower, and was bringing up his daughter, on his side, in the same severe seclusion in which I was spending my days. To this day I am unacquainted with the origin of the bond of union between our respective progenitors. Mr. Vernor was largely engaged in business, and I imagine that once upon a time he found himself in a financial strait and was helped through it by my father's coming forward with a heavy loan, on which, in his situation, he could offer no security but his word. Of this my father was quite capable. He was a man of dogmas, and he was sure to have a rule of life—as clear as if it had been written out in his beautiful copper-plate hand—adapted to the conduct of a gentleman toward a friend in pecuniary embarrassment. What is more, he was sure to adhere to it. Mr. Vernor, I believe, got on his feet, paid his debt, and vowed my father an eternal gratitude. His little daughter was the apple of his eye, and he pledged himself to bring her up to be the wife of his benefactor's son. So our fate was fixed, parentally, and we have been educated for each other. I have not seen my betrothed since she was a very plain-faced little girl in a sticky pinafore, hugging a one-armed doll—of the male sex, I believe—as big as herself. Mr. Vernor is in what is called the Eastern trade, and has been living these many years at Smyrna. Isabel has grown up there in a white-walled garden, in an orange grove, between her father and her governess. She is a good deal my junior; six months ago she was seventeen; when she is eighteen we are to marry."

He related all this calmly enough, without the accent of complaint, drily rather and doggedly, as if he were weary of thinking of it. "It's a romance, indeed, for these dull days," I said, "and I heartily congratulate you. It's not every young man who finds, on reaching the marrying age, a wife kept in a box of rose-leaves for him. A thousand to one Miss Vernor is charming; I wonder you don't post off to Smyrna."

"You are joking," he answered, with a wounded air, "and I am terribly serious. Let me tell you the rest. I never suspected this superior conspiracy till something less than a year ago. My father, wishing to provide against his death, informed me of it very solemnly. I was neither elated nor depressed; I received it, as I remember, with a sort of emotion which varied only in degree from that with which I could have hailed the announcement that he had ordered me a set of new shirts. I supposed that was the way that all marriages were made; I had heard of their being made in heaven, and what was my father but a divinity? Novels and poems,

                                                  EUGENE PICKERING

indeed, talked about falling in love; but novels and poems were one thing and life was another. A short time afterwards he introduced me to a photograph of my predestined, who has a pretty, but an extremely inanimate, face. After this his health failed rapidly. One night I was sitting, as I habitually sat for hours, in his dimly-lighted room, near his bed, to which he had been confined for a week. He had not spoken for some time, and I supposed he was asleep; but happening to look at him I saw his eyes wide open, and fixed on me strangely. He was smiling benignantly, intensely, and in a moment he beckoned to me. Then, on my going to him—'I feel that I shall not last long,' he said; 'but I am willing to die when I think how comfortably I have arranged your future.' He was talking of death, and anything but grief at that moment was doubtless impious and monstrous; but there came into my heart for the first time a throbbing sense of being over-governed. I said nothing, and he thought my silence was all sorrow. 'I shall not live to see you married,' he went on, 'but since the foundation is laid, that little signifies; it would be a selfish pleasure, and I have never thought of myself but in you. To foresee your future, in its main outline, to know to a certainty that you will be safely domiciled here, with a wife approved by my judgment, cultivating the moral fruit of which I have sown the seed—this will content me. But, my son, I wish to clear this bright vision from the shadow of a doubt. I believe in your docility; I believe I may trust the salutary force of your respect for my memory. But I must remember that when I am removed you will stand here alone, face to face with a hundred nameless temptations to perversity. The fumes of unrighteous pride may rise into your brain and tempt you, in the interest of a vulgar theory which it will call your independence, to shatter the edifice I have so laboriously constructed. So I must ask you for a promise—the solemn promise you owe my condition.' And he grasped my hand. 'You will follow the path I have marked; you will be faithful to the young girl whom an influence as devoted as that which has governed your own young life has moulded into everything amiable; you will marry Isabel Vernor.' This was pretty 'steep,' as we used to say at school. I was frightened; I drew away my hand and asked to be trusted without any such terrible vow. My reluctance startled my father into a suspicion that the vulgar theory of independence had already been whispering to me. He sat up in his bed and looked at me with eyes which seemed to foresee a lifetime of odious ingratitude. I felt the reproach; I feel it now. I promised! And even now I don't regret my promise nor complain of my father's tenacity. I feel, somehow, as if the seeds of ultimate repose had been sown in those unsuspecting years—as if after many days I might gather the mellow fruit. But after many days! I will keep my promise, I will obey; but I want to *live* first!"

"My dear fellow, you are living now. All this passionate consciousness of your situation is a very ardent life. I wish I could say as much for my own."

"I want to forget my situation. I want to spend three months without thinking of the past or the future, grasping whatever the present offers me. Yesterday I thought I was in a fair way to sail with the tide. But this morning comes this memento!" And he held up his letter again.

"What is it?"

"A letter from Smyrna."

"I see you have not yet broken the seal."

"No; nor do I mean to, for the present. It contains bad news."

"What do you call bad news?"

"News that I am expected in Smyrna in three weeks. News that Mr. Vernor disapproves of my roving about the world. News that his daughter is standing expectant at the altar."

"Is not this pure conjecture?"

"Conjecture, possibly, but safe conjecture. As soon as I looked at the letter something smote me at the heart. Look at the device on the seal, and I am sure you will find it's *Tarry not*!" And he flung the letter on the grass.

"Upon my word, you had better open it," I said.

"If I were to open it and read my summons, do you know what I should do? I should march home and ask the Oberkellner how one gets to Smyrna, pack my trunk, take my ticket, and not stop till I arrived. I know I should; it would be the fascination of habit. The only way, therefore, to wander to my rope's end is to leave the letter unread."

"In your place," I said, "curiosity would make me open it."

He shook his head. "I have no curiosity! For a long time now the idea of my marriage has ceased to be a novelty, and I have contemplated it mentally in every possible light. I fear nothing from that side, but I do fear something from conscience. I want my hands tied. Will you do me a favour? Pick up the letter, put it into your pocket, and keep it till I ask you for it. When I do, you may know that I am at my rope's end."

I took the letter, smiling. "And how long is your rope to be? The Homburg season doesn't last for ever."

"Does it last a month? Let that be my season! A month hence you will give it back to me."

"To-morrow if you say so. Meanwhile, let it rest in peace!" And I consigned it to the most sacred interstice of my pocket-book. To say that I was disposed to humour the poor fellow would seem to be saying that I thought his request fantastic. It was his situation, by no fault of his own, that was fantastic, and he was only trying to be natural. He watched me put away the letter, and when it had disappeared gave a soft sigh of relief. The sigh was natural, and yet it set me thinking. His general recoil from an immediate responsibility imposed by others might be wholesome enough; but if there was an old grievance on one side, was there not possibly a new-born delusion on the other? It would be unkind to withhold a reflection that might serve as a warning; so I told him, abruptly, that I had been an undiscovered spectator, the night before, of his exploits at roulette.

He blushed deeply, but he met my eyes with the same clear good-humour.

"Ah, then, you saw that wonderful lady?"

"Wonderful she was indeed. I saw her afterwards, too, sitting on the terrace in the starlight. I imagine she was not alone."

"No, indeed, I was with her—for nearly an hour. Then I walked home with her."

"Ah! And did you go in?"

"No, she said it was too late to ask me; though she remarked that in a general way she did not stand upon ceremony."

"She did herself injustice. When it came to losing your money for you, she made you insist."

"Ah, you noticed that too?" cried Pickering, still quite unconfused. "I felt as if the whole table were staring at me; but her manner was so gracious and reassuring that I supposed she was doing nothing unusual. She confessed, however, afterwards, that she is very eccentric. The world began to call her so, she said, before she ever dreamed of it, and at last finding that she had the reputation, in spite of herself, she resolved to enjoy its privileges. Now, she does what she chooses."

"In other words, she is a lady with no reputation to lose!"

Pickering seemed puzzled; he smiled a little. "Is not that what you say of bad women?"

"Of some—of those who are found out."

"Well," he said, still smiling, "I have not yet found out Madame Blumenthal."

"If that's her name, I suppose she's German."

"Yes; but she speaks English so well that you wouldn't know it. She is very clever. Her husband is dead."

I laughed involuntarily at the conjunction of these facts, and Pickering's clear glance seemed to question my mirth. "You have been so bluntly frank with me," I said, "that I too must be frank. Tell me, if you can, whether this clever Madame Blumenthal, whose husband is dead, has given a point to your desire for a suspension of communication with Smyrna."

He seemed to ponder my question, unshrinkingly. "I think not," he said, at last. "I have had the desire for three months; I have known Madame Blumenthal for less than twenty-four hours."

"Very true. But when you found this letter of yours on your place at breakfast, did you seem for a moment to see Madame Blumenthal sitting opposite?"

"Opposite?"

"Opposite, my dear fellow, or anywhere in the neighbourhood. In a word, does she interest you?"

"Very much!" he cried, joyously.

"Amen!" I answered, jumping up with a laugh. "And now, if we are to see the world in a month, there is no time to lose. Let us begin with the Hardtwald."

Pickering rose, and we strolled away into the forest, talking of lighter things. At last we reached the edge of the wood, sat down on a fallen log, and looked out across an interval of meadow at the long wooded waves of the Taunus. What my friend was thinking of I can't say; I was meditating on his queer biography, and letting my wonderment wander away to Smyrna. Suddenly I remembered that he possessed a portrait of the young girl who was waiting for him there in a white-walled garden. I asked him if he had it with him. He said nothing, but gravely took out his pocket-book and drew forth a small photograph. It represented, as the poet says, a simple maiden in her flower—a slight young girl, with a certain childish roundness of contour. There was no ease in her posture; she was standing, stiffly and shyly, for her likeness; she wore a short-waisted white dress; her arms hung at her sides and her hands were clasped in front; her head was bent downward a little, and her dark eyes fixed. But her awkwardness was as pretty as that of some angular seraph in a mediæval carving, and in her timid gaze there seemed to lurk the questioning gleam of childhood. "What is this for?" her charming eyes appeared to ask; "why have I been dressed up for this ceremony in a white frock and amber beads?"

"Gracious powers!" I said to myself; "what an enchanting thing is innocence!"

"That portrait was taken a year and a half ago," said Pickering, as if with an effort to be perfectly just. "By this time, I suppose, she looks a little wiser."

"Not much, I hope," I said, as I gave it back. "She is very sweet!"

"Yes, poor girl, she is very sweet—no doubt!" And he put the thing away without looking at it.

We were silent for some moments. At last, abruptly—"My dear fellow," I said, "I should take some satisfaction in seeing you immediately leave Homburg."

"Immediately?"

"To-day—as soon as you can get ready."

He looked at me, surprised, and little by little he blushed. "There is something I have not told you," he said; "something that your saying that Madame Blumenthal has no reputation to lose has made me half afraid to tell you."

"I think I can guess it. Madame Blumenthal has asked you to come and play her game for her again."

"Not at all!" cried Pickering, with a smile of triumph. "She says that she means to play no more for the present. She has asked me to come and take tea with her this evening."

"Ah, then," I said, very gravely, "of course you can't leave Homburg."

He answered nothing, but looked askance at me, as if he were expecting me to laugh. "Urge it strongly," he said in a moment. "Say it's my duty—that I *must*."

I didn't quite understand him, but, feathering the shaft with a harmless expletive, I told him that unless he followed my advice I would never speak to him again.

He got up, stood before me, and struck the ground with his stick. "Good!" he cried; "I wanted an occasion to break a rule—to leap a barrier. Here it is. I stay!"

I made him a mock bow for his energy. "That's very fine," I said; "but now, to put you in a proper mood for Madame Blumenthal's tea, we will go and listen to the band play Schubert under the lindens." And we walked back through the woods.

I went to see Pickering the next day, at his inn, and on knocking, as directed, at his door, was surprised to hear the sound of a loud voice within. My knock remained unnoticed, so I presently introduced myself. I found no company, but I discovered my friend walking up and down the room and apparently declaiming to himself from a little volume bound in white vellum. He greeted me heartily, threw his book on the table, and said that he was taking a German lesson.

"And who is your teacher?" I asked, glancing at the book.

He rather avoided meeting my eye, as he answered, after an instant's delay, "Madame Blumenthal."

"Indeed! Has she written a grammar?"

"It's not a grammar; it's a tragedy." And he handed me the book.

I opened it, and beheld, in delicate type, with a very large margin, an *Historisches Trauerspiel* in five acts, entitled "Cleopatra." There were a great many marginal corrections and annotations, apparently from the author's hand; the speeches were very long, and there was an inordinate number of soliloquies by the heroine. One of them, I remember, towards the end of the play, began in this fashion—

"What, after all, is life but sensation, and sensation but deception?—reality that pales before the light of one's dreams as Octavia's dull beauty fades beside mine? But let me believe in some intenser bliss, and seek it in the arms of death!"

"It seems decidedly passionate," I said. "Has the tragedy ever been acted?"

"Never in public; but Madame Blumenthal tells me that she had it played at her own house in Berlin, and that she herself undertook the part of the heroine."

Pickering's unworldly life had not been of a sort to sharpen his perception of the ridiculous, but it seemed to me an unmistakable sign of his being under the charm, that this information was very soberly offered. He was preoccupied, he was irresponsive to my experimental observations on vulgar topics—the hot weather, the inn, the advent of Adelina Patti. At last, uttering his thoughts, he announced that Madame Blumenthal had proved to be an extraordinarily interesting woman. He seemed to have quite forgotten our long talk in the Hartwaldt, and betrayed no sense of this being a confession that he had taken his plunge and was floating with the current. He only remembered that I had spoken slightingly of the lady, and he now hinted that it behoved me to amend my opinion. I had received the day before so strong an impression of a sort of spiritual fastidiousness in my friend's nature, that on hearing now the striking of a new hour, as it were, in his consciousness, and observing how the echoes of the past were immediately quenched in its music, I said to myself that it had certainly taken a delicate hand to wind up that fine machine. No doubt Madame Blumenthal was a clever woman. It is a good German custom at Homburg to spend the hour preceding dinner in listening to the orchestra in the Kurgarten; Mozart and Beethoven, for organisms in which the interfusion of soul and sense is peculiarly mysterious, are a vigorous stimulus to the appetite. Pickering and I conformed, as we had done the day before, to the fashion, and when we were seated under the trees, he began to expatiate on his friend's merits.

"I don't know whether she is eccentric or not," he said; "to me every one seems eccentric, and it's not for me, yet a while, to measure people by my narrow precedents. I never saw a gaming table in my life before, and supposed that a gambler was of necessity some dusky villain with an evil eye. In Germany, says Madame Blumenthal, people play at roulette as they play at billiards, and her own venerable mother originally taught her the rules of the game. It is a recognised source of subsistence for decent people with small means. But I confess Madame Blumenthal might do worse things than play at roulette, and yet make them harmonious and beautiful. I have never been in the habit of thinking positive beauty the most excellent thing in a woman. I have always said to myself that if my heart were ever to be captured it would be by a sort of general grace—a sweetness of motion and tone—on which one could count for soothing impressions, as one counts on a musical instrument that is perfectly in tune. Madame Blumenthal has it— this grace that soothes and satisfies; and it seems the more perfect that it keeps order and harmony in a character really passionately ardent and active. With her eager nature and her innumerable accomplishments nothing would be easier than that she should seem restless and aggressive. You will know her, and I leave you to judge whether she does seem so! She has every gift, and culture has done everything for each. What goes on in her mind I of course can't say; what reaches the observer—the admirer—is simply a sort of fragrant emanation of intelligence and sympathy."

"Madame Blumenthal," I said, smiling, "might be the loveliest woman in the world, and you the object of her choicest favours, and yet what I should most envy you would be, not your peerless friend, but your beautiful imagination."

"That's a polite way of calling me a fool," said Pickering. "You are a sceptic, a cynic, a satirist! I hope I shall be a long time coming to that."

"You will make the journey fast if you travel by express trains. But pray tell me, have you ventured to intimate to Madame Blumenthal your high opinion of her?"

"I don't know what I may have said. She listens even better than she talks, and I think it possible I may have made her listen to a great deal of nonsense. For after the first few words I exchanged with her I was conscious of an extraordinary evaporation of all my old diffidence. I have, in truth, I suppose," he added in a moment, "owing to my peculiar circumstances, a great accumulated fund of unuttered things of all sorts to get rid of. Last evening, sitting there before that charming woman, they came swarming to my lips. Very likely I poured them all out. I have a sense of having enshrouded myself in a sort of mist of talk, and of seeing her lovely eyes shining through it opposite to me, like fog-lamps at sea." And here, if I remember rightly, Pickering broke off into an ardent parenthesis, and declared that Madame Blumenthal's eyes had something in them that he had never seen in any others. "It was a jumble of crudities and inanities," he went on; "they must have seemed to her great rubbish; but I felt the wiser and the stronger, somehow, for having fired off all my guns—they could hurt nobody now if they hit—and I imagine I might have gone far without finding another woman in whom such an exhibition would have provoked so little of mere cold amusement."

"Madame Blumenthal, on the contrary," I surmised, "entered into your situation with warmth."

"Exactly so—the greatest! She has felt and suffered, and now she understands!"

"She told you, I imagine, that she understood you as if she had made you, and she offered to be your guide, philosopher, and friend."

"She spoke to me," Pickering answered, after a pause, "as I had never been spoken to before, and she offered me, formally, all the offices of a woman's friendship."

"Which you as formally accepted?"

"To you the scene sounds absurd, I suppose, but allow me to say I don't care!" Pickering spoke with an air of genial defiance which was the most inoffensive thing in the world. "I was very much moved; I was, in fact, very much excited. I tried to say something, but I couldn't; I had had plenty to say before, but now I stammered and bungled, and at last I bolted out of the room."

"Meanwhile she had dropped her tragedy into your pocket!"

"Not at all. I had seen it on the table before she came in. Afterwards she kindly offered to read German aloud with me, for the accent, two or three times a week. 'What shall we begin with?' she asked. 'With this!' I said, and held up the book. And she let me take it to look it over."

I was neither a cynic nor a satirist, but even if I had been, I might have been disarmed by Pickering's assurance, before we parted, that Madame Blumenthal wished to know me and expected him to introduce me. Among the foolish things which, according to his own account, he had uttered, were some generous words in my praise, to which she had civilly replied. I confess I was curious to see her, but I begged that the introduction should not be immediate, for I wished to let Pickering work out his destiny alone. For some days I saw little of him, though we met at the Kursaal and strolled occasionally in the park. I watched, in spite of my desire to let him alone, for the signs and portents of the world's action upon him—of that portion of the world, in especial, of which Madame Blumenthal had constituted herself the agent. He seemed very happy, and gave me in a dozen ways an impression of increased self-confidence and maturity. His mind was admirably active, and always, after a quarter of an hour's talk with him, I asked myself what experience could really do, that innocence had not done, to make it bright and fine. I was struck with his deep enjoyment of the whole spectacle of foreign life— its novelty, its picturesqueness, its light and shade—and with the infinite freedom with which he felt he could go and come and rove and linger and observe it all. It was an expansion, an awakening, a coming to moral manhood. Each time I met him he spoke a little less of Madame Blumenthal; but he let me know generally that he saw her often, and continued to admire her. I was forced to admit to myself, in spite of preconceptions, that if she were really the ruling star of this happy season, she must be a very superior woman. Pickering had the air of an ingenuous young philosopher sitting at the feet of an austere muse, and not of a sentimental spendthrift dangling about some supreme incarnation of levity.

CHAPTER II

Madame Blumenthal seemed, for the time, to have abjured the Kursaal, and I never caught a glimpse of her. Her young friend, apparently, was an interesting study, and the studious mind prefers seclusion.

She reappeared, however, at last, one evening at the opera, where from my chair I perceived her in a box, looking extremely pretty. Adelina Patti was singing, and after the rising of the curtain I was occupied with the stage; but on looking round when it fell for the *entr'acte*, I saw that the authoress of "Cleopatra" had been joined by her young admirer. He was sitting a little behind her, leaning forward, looking over her shoulder and listening, while she, slowly moving her fan to and fro and letting her eye wander over the house, was apparently talking of this person and that. No doubt she was saying sharp things; but Pickering was not laughing; his eyes were following her covert indications; his mouth was half open, as it always was when he was interested; he looked intensely serious. I was glad that, having her back to him, she was unable to see how he looked. It seemed the proper moment to present myself and make her my bow; but just as I was about to leave my place a gentleman, whom in a moment I perceived to be an old acquaintance, came to occupy the next chair. Recognition and mutual greetings followed, and I was forced to postpone my visit to Madame Blumenthal. I was not sorry, for it very soon occurred to me that Niedermeyer would be just the man to give me a fair prose version of Pickering's lyric tributes to his friend. He was an Austrian by birth, and had formerly lived about Europe a great deal in a series of small diplomatic posts. England especially he had often visited, and he spoke the language almost without accent. I had once spent three rainy days with him in the house of an English friend in the country. He was a sharp observer, and a good deal of a gossip; he knew a little something about every one, and about some people everything. His knowledge on social matters generally had the quality of all German science; it was copious, minute, exhaustive.

"Do tell me," I said, as we stood looking round the house, "who and what is the lady in white, with the young man sitting behind her."

"Who?" he answered, dropping his glass. "Madame Blumenthal! What! It would take long to say. Be introduced; it's easily done; you will find her charming. Then, after a week, you will tell me what she is."

"Perhaps I should not. My friend there has known her a week, and I don't think he is yet able to give a coherent account of her."

He raised his glass again, and after looking a while, "I am afraid your friend is a little—what do you call it?—a little 'soft.' Poor fellow! he's not the first. I have never known this lady that she has not had some eligible youth hovering about in some such attitude as that, undergoing the softening process. She looks wonderfully well, from here. It's extraordinary how those women last!"

"You don't mean, I take it, when you talk about 'those women,' that Madame Blumenthal is not embalmed, for duration, in a certain infusion of respectability?"

"Yes and no. The atmosphere that surrounds her is entirely of her own making. There is no reason in her antecedents that people should drop their voice when they speak of her. But some women are never at their ease till they have given some damnable twist or other to their position before the world. The attitude of upright virtue is unbecoming, like sitting too straight in a fauteuil. Don't ask me for opinions, however; content yourself with a few facts and with an anecdote. Madame Blumenthal is Prussian, and very well born. I remember her mother, an old Westphalian

                                        EUGENE PICKERING

Gräfin, with principles marshalled out like Frederick the Great's grenadiers. She was poor, however, and her principles were an insufficient dowry for Anastasia, who was married very young to a vicious Jew, twice her own age. He was supposed to have money, but I am afraid he had less than was nominated in the bond, or else that his pretty young wife spent it very fast. She has been a widow these six or eight years, and has lived, I imagine, in rather a hand-to-mouth fashion. I suppose she is some six or eight and thirty years of age. In winter one hears of her in Berlin, giving little suppers to the artistic rabble there; in summer one often sees her across the green table at Ems and Wiesbaden. She's very clever, and her cleverness has spoiled her. A year after her marriage she published a novel, with her views on matrimony, in the George Sand manner—beating the drum to Madame Sand's trumpet. No doubt she was very unhappy; Blumenthal was an old beast. Since then she has published a lot of literature—novels and poems and pamphlets on every conceivable theme, from the conversion of Lola Montez to the Hegelian philosophy. Her talk is much better than her writing. Her *conjugophobia*—I can't call it by any other name—made people think lightly of her at a time when her rebellion against marriage was probably only theoretic. She had a taste for spinning fine phrases, she drove her shuttle, and when she came to the end of her yarn she found that society had turned its back. She tossed her head, declared that at last she could breathe the sacred air of freedom, and formally announced that she had embraced an 'intellectual' life. This meant unlimited *camaraderie* with scribblers and daubers, Hegelian philosophers and Hungarian pianists. But she has been admired also by a great many really clever men; there was a time, in fact, when she turned a head as well set on its shoulders as this one!" And Niedermeyer tapped his forehead. "She has a great charm, and, literally, I know no harm of her. Yet for all that, I am not going to speak to her; I am not going near her box. I am going to leave her to say, if she does me the honour to observe the omission, that I too have gone over to the Philistines. It's not that; it is that there is something sinister about the woman. I am too old for it to frighten me, but I am good-natured enough for it to pain me. Her quarrel with society has brought her no happiness, and her outward charm is only the mask of a dangerous discontent. Her imagination is lodged where her heart should be! So long as you amuse it, well and good; she's radiant. But the moment you let it flag, she is capable of dropping you without a pang. If you land on your feet you are so much the wiser, simply; but there have been two or three, I believe, who have almost broken their necks in the fall."

"You are reversing your promise," I said, "and giving me an opinion, but not an anecdote."

"This is my anecdote. A year ago a friend of mine made her acquaintance in Berlin, and though he was no longer a young man, and had never been what is called a susceptible one, he took a great fancy to Madame Blumenthal. He's a major in the Prussian artillery—grizzled, grave, a trifle severe, a man every way firm in the faith of his fathers. It's a proof of Anastasia's charm that such a man should have got into the habit of going to see her every day of his life. But the major was in love, or next door to it! Every day that he called he found her scribbling away at a little ormolu table on a lot of half-sheets of note-paper. She used to bid him sit down and hold his tongue for a quarter of an hour, till she had finished her chapter; she was writing a novel, and it was promised to a publisher. Clorinda, she confided to him, was the name of the injured heroine. The major, I imagine, had never read a work of fiction in his life, but he knew by hearsay that Madame Blumenthal's literature, when put forth in pink covers, was subversive of several respectable institutions. Besides, he didn't believe in women knowing how to write at all, and it irritated him to see this inky goddess correcting proof-sheets under his nose—irritated him the more that, as I say, he was in love with her and that he ventured to believe she had a kindness for his years and his honours. And yet she was not such a woman as he could easily ask to marry him. The result of all this was that he fell into the way of railing at her intellectual pursuits and saying he should like to run his sword through her pile of papers. A woman was clever enough when she could guess her husband's wishes, and learned enough when she could read him the newspapers. At last, one day, Madame Blumenthal flung down her pen and announced in triumph that she had finished her novel. Clorinda had expired in the arms of—some one else than her husband. The major, by way of congratulating her, declared that her novel was immoral rubbish, and that her love of vicious paradoxes was only a peculiarly depraved form of coquetry. He added, however, that he loved her in spite of her follies, and that if she would formally abjure them he would as formally offer her his hand. They say that women like to be snubbed by military men. I don't know, I'm sure; I don't know how much pleasure, on this occasion, was mingled with Anastasia's wrath. But her wrath was very quiet, and the major assured me it made her look uncommonly pretty. 'I have told you before,' she says, 'that I write from an inner need. I write to unburden my heart, to satisfy my conscience. You call my poor efforts coquetry, vanity, the desire to produce a sensation. I can prove to you that it is the quiet labour itself I care for, and not the world's more or less flattering attention to it!' And seizing the history of Clorinda she thrust it into the fire. The major stands staring, and the first thing he knows she is sweeping him a great curtsey and bidding him farewell for ever. Left alone and recovering his wits, he fishes out Clorinda from the embers, and then proceeds to thump vigorously at the lady's door. But it never opened, and from that day to the day three months ago when he told me the tale, he had not beheld her again."

"By Jove, it's a striking story," I said. "But the question is, what does it prove?"

"Several things. First (what I was careful not to tell my friend), that Madame Blumenthal cared for him a trifle more than he supposed; second, that he cares for her more than ever; third, that the performance was a master-stroke, and that her allowing him to force an interview upon her again is only a question of time."

"And last?" I asked.

"This is another anecdote. The other day, Unter den Linden, I saw on a bookseller's counter a little pink-covered romance— 'Sophronia,' by Madame Blumenthal. Glancing through it, I observed an extraordinary abuse of asterisks; every two or three pages the narrative was adorned with a portentous blank, crossed with a row of stars."

"Well, but poor Clorinda?" I objected, as Niedermeyer paused.

"Sophronia, my dear fellow, is simply Clorinda renamed by the baptism of fire. The fair author came back, of course, and found Clorinda tumbled upon the floor, a good deal scorched, but, on the whole, more frightened than hurt. She picks her up, brushes her off, and sends her to the printer. Wherever the flames had burnt a hole she swings a constellation! But if the major is prepared to drop a penitent tear over the ashes of Clorinda, I shall not whisper to him that the urn is empty."

Even Adelina Patti's singing, for the next half-hour, but half availed to divert me from my quickened curiosity to behold Madame Blumenthal face to face. As soon as the curtain had fallen again I repaired to her box and was ushered in by Pickering with zealous hospitality. His glowing smile seemed to say to me, "Ay, look for yourself, and adore!" Nothing could have been more gracious than the lady's greeting, and I found, somewhat to my surprise, that her prettiness lost nothing on a nearer view. Her eyes indeed were the finest I have ever seen—the softest, the deepest, the most intensely responsive. In spite of something faded and jaded in her physiognomy, her movements, her smile, and the tone of her voice, especially when she laughed, had an almost girlish frankness and spontaneity. She looked at you very hard with her radiant gray eyes, and she indulged while she talked in a superabundance of restless, rather affected little gestures, as if to make you take her meaning in a certain very particular and superfine sense. I wondered whether after a while this might not fatigue one's attention; then meeting her charming eyes, I said, Not for a long time. She was very clever, and, as Pickering had said, she spoke English admirably. I told her, as I took my seat beside her, of the fine things I had heard about her from my friend, and she listened, letting me go on some time, and exaggerate a little, with her fine eyes fixed full upon me. "Really?" she suddenly said, turning short round upon Pickering, who stood behind us, and looking at him in the same way. "Is that the way you talk about me?"

He blushed to his eyes, and I repented. She suddenly began to laugh; it was then I observed how sweet her voice was in laughter. We talked after this of various matters, and in a little while I complimented her on her excellent English, and asked if she had learnt it in England.

"Heaven forbid!" she cried. "I have never been there and wish never to go. I should never get on with the—" I wondered what she was going to say; the fogs, the smoke, or whist with sixpenny stakes?—"I should never get on," she said, "with the aristocracy! I am a fierce democrat—I am not ashamed of it. I hold opinions which would make my ancestors turn in their graves. I was born in the lap of feudalism. I am a daughter of the crusaders. But I am a revolutionist! I have a passion for freedom—my idea of happiness is to die on a great barricade! It's to your great country I should like to go. I should like to see the wonderful spectacle of a great people free to do everything it chooses, and yet never doing anything wrong!"

I replied, modestly, that, after all, both our freedom and our good conduct had their limits, and she turned quickly about and shook her fan with a dramatic gesture at Pickering. "No matter, no matter!" she cried; "I should like to see the country which produced that wonderful young man. I think of it as a sort of Arcadia—a land of the golden age. He's so delightfully innocent! In this stupid old Germany, if a young man is innocent he's a fool; he has no brains; he's not a bit interesting. But Mr. Pickering says the freshest things, and after I have laughed five minutes at their freshness it suddenly occurs to me that they are very wise, and I think them over for a week." "True!" she went on, nodding at him. "I call them inspired solecisms, and I treasure them up. Remember that when I next laugh at you!"

Glancing at Pickering, I was prompted to believe that he was in a state of beatific exaltation which weighed Madame Blumenthal's smiles and frowns in an equal balance. They were equally hers; they were links alike in the golden chain. He looked at me with eyes that seemed to say, "Did you ever hear such wit? Did you ever see such grace?" It seemed to me that he was but vaguely conscious of the meaning of her words; her gestures, her voice and glance, made an absorbing harmony. There is something painful in the spectacle of absolute enthralment, even to an excellent cause. I gave no response to Pickering's challenge, but made some remark upon the charm of Adelina Patti's singing. Madame Blumenthal, as became a "revolutionist," was obliged to confess that she could see no charm in it; it was meagre, it was trivial, it lacked soul. "You must know that in music, too," she said, "I think for myself!" And she began with a great many flourishes of her fan to explain what it was she thought. Remarkable things, doubtless; but I cannot answer for it, for in the midst of the explanation the curtain rose again. "You can't be a great artist without a great passion!" Madame Blumenthal was affirming. Before I had time to assent Madame Patti's voice rose wheeling like a skylark, and rained down its silver notes. "Ah, give me that art," I whispered, "and I will leave you your passion!" And I departed for my own place in the orchestra. I wondered afterwards whether the speech had seemed rude, and inferred that it had not on receiving a friendly nod from the lady, in the lobby, as the theatre was emptying itself. She was on Pickering's arm, and he was taking her to her carriage. Distances are short in Homburg, but the night was rainy, and Madame Blumenthal exhibited a very pretty satin-shod foot as a reason why, though but a penniless widow, she should not walk home. Pickering left us together a moment while he went to hail the vehicle, and my companion seized the opportunity, as she said, to beg me to be so very kind as to come and see her. It was for a particular reason! It was reason enough for me, of course, I answered, that she had given me leave. She looked at me a moment with that extraordinary gaze of hers which seemed so absolutely audacious in its candour, and rejoined that I paid more compliments than our young friend there, but that she was sure I was not half so sincere. "But it's about him I want to talk," she said. "I want to ask you many things; I want you to tell me all about him. He interests me; but you see my sympathies are so intense, my imagination is so lively, that I don't trust my own impressions. They have misled me more than once!" And she gave a little tragic shudder.

I promised to come and compare notes with her, and we bade her farewell at her carriage door. Pickering and I remained a while, walking up and down the long glazed gallery of the Kursaal. I had not taken many steps before I became aware that I was beside a man in the very extremity of love. "Isn't she wonderful?" he asked, with an implicit confidence in my sympathy which it cost me some ingenuity to elude. If he were really in love, well and good! For although, now that I had seen her, I stood ready to confess to large possibilities of fascination on Madame Blumenthal's part, and even to certain possibilities of sincerity of which my appreciation was vague, yet it seemed to me less ominous that he should be simply smitten than that his admiration should pique itself on being discriminating. It was on his fundamental simplicity that I counted for a happy termination of his experiment, and the former of these alternatives seemed to me the simpler. I resolved to hold my tongue and let him run his course. He had a great deal to say about his happiness, about the days passing like hours, the hours like minutes, and about Madame Blumenthal being a "revelation." "She was nothing to-night," he said; "nothing to what she sometimes is in the way of brilliancy—in the way of repartee. If you could only hear her when she tells her adventures!"

"Adventures?" I inquired. "Has she had adventures?"

"Of the most wonderful sort!" cried Pickering, with rapture. "She hasn't vegetated, like me! She has lived in the tumult of life. When I listen to her reminiscences, it's like hearing the opening tumult of one of Beethoven's symphonies as it loses itself in a triumphant harmony of beauty and faith!"

I could only lift my eyebrows, but I desired to know before we separated what he had done with that troublesome conscience of his. "I suppose you know, my dear fellow," I said, "that you are simply in love. That's what they happen to call your state of mind."

He replied with a brightening eye, as if he were delighted to hear it—"So Madame Blumenthal told me only this morning!" And seeing, I suppose, that I was slightly puzzled, "I went to drive with her," he continued; "we drove to Königstein, to see the old castle. We scrambled up into the heart of the ruin and sat for an hour in one of the crumbling old courts. Something in the solemn stillness of the place unloosed my tongue; and while she sat on an ivied stone, on the edge of the plunging wall, I stood there and made a speech. She listened to me, looking at me, breaking off little bits of stone and letting them drop down into the valley. At last she got up and nodded at me two or three times silently, with a smile, as if she were applauding me for a solo on the violin. 'You are in love,' she said. 'It's a perfect case!' And for some time she said nothing more. But before we left the place she told me that she owed me an answer to my speech. She thanked me heartily, but she was afraid that if she took me at my word she would be taking advantage of my inexperience. I had known few women; I was too easily pleased; I thought her better than she really was. She had great faults; I must know her longer and find them out; I must compare her with other women—women younger, simpler, more innocent, more ignorant; and then if I still did her the honour to think well of her, she would listen to me again. I told her that I was not afraid of preferring any woman in the world to her, and then she repeated, 'Happy man, happy man! you are in love, you are in love!'"

                                              EUGENE PICKERING

I called upon Madame Blumenthal a couple of days later, in some agitation of thought. It has been proved that there are, here and there, in the world, such people as sincere impostors; certain characters who cultivate fictitious emotions in perfect good faith. Even if this clever lady enjoyed poor Pickering's bedazzlement, it was conceivable that, taking vanity and charity together, she should care more for his welfare than for her own entertainment; and her offer to abide by the result of hazardous comparison with other women was a finer stroke than her reputation had led me to expect. She received me in a shabby little sitting-room littered with uncut books and newspapers, many of which I saw at a glance were French. One side of it was occupied by an open piano, surmounted by a jar full of white roses. They perfumed the air; they seemed to me to exhale the pure aroma of Pickering's devotion. Buried in an arm-chair, the object of this devotion was reading the *Revue des Deux Mondes*. The purpose of my visit was not to admire Madame Blumenthal on my own account, but to ascertain how far I might safely leave her to work her will upon my friend. She had impugned my sincerity the evening of the opera, and I was careful on this occasion to abstain from compliments, and not to place her on her guard against my penetration. It is needless to narrate our interview in detail; indeed, to tell the perfect truth, I was punished for my rash attempt to surprise her by a temporary eclipse of my own perspicacity. She sat there so questioning, so perceptive, so genial, so generous, and so pretty withal, that I was quite ready at the end of half an hour to subscribe to the most comprehensive of Pickering's rhapsodies. She was certainly a wonderful woman. I have never liked to linger, in memory, on that half-hour. The result of it was to prove that there were many more things in the composition of a woman who, as Niedermeyer said, had lodged her imagination in the place of her heart than were dreamt of in my philosophy. Yet, as I sat there stroking my hat and balancing the account between nature and art in my affable hostess, I felt like a very competent philosopher. She had said she wished me to tell her everything about our friend, and she questioned me as to his family, his fortune, his antecedents, and his character. All this was natural in a woman who had received a passionate declaration of love, and it was expressed with an air of charmed solicitude, a radiant confidence that there was really no mistake about his being a most distinguished young man, and that if I chose to be explicit, I might deepen her conviction to disinterested ecstasy, which might have almost provoked me to invent a good opinion, if I had not had one ready made. I told her that she really knew Pickering better than I did, and that until we met at Homburg I had not seen him since he was a boy.

"But he talks to you freely," she answered; "I know you are his confidant. He has told me certainly a great many things, but I always feel as if he were keeping something back; as if he were holding something behind him, and showing me only one hand at once. He seems often to be hovering on the edge of a secret. I have had several friendships in my life—thank Heaven! but I have had none more dear to me than this one. Yet in the midst of it I have the painful sense of my friend being half afraid of me; of his thinking me terrible, strange, perhaps a trifle out of my wits. Poor me! If he only knew what a plain good soul I am, and how I only want to know him and befriend him!"

These words were full of a plaintive magnanimity which made mistrust seem cruel. How much better I might play providence over Pickering's experiments with life if I could engage the fine instincts of this charming woman on the providential side! Pickering's secret was, of course, his engagement to Miss Vernor; it was natural enough that he should have been unable to bring himself to talk of it to Madame Blumenthal. The simple sweetness of this young girl's face had not faded from my memory; I could not rid myself of the suspicion that in going further Pickering might fare much worse. Madame Blumenthal's professions seemed a virtual promise to agree with me, and, after some hesitation, I said that my friend had, in fact, a substantial secret, and that perhaps I might do him a good turn by putting her in possession of it. In as few words as possible I told her that Pickering stood pledged by filial piety to marry a young lady at Smyrna. She listened intently to my story; when I had finished it there was a faint flush of excitement in each of her cheeks. She broke out into a dozen exclamations of admiration and compassion. "What a wonderful tale—what a romantic situation! No wonder poor Mr. Pickering seemed restless and unsatisfied; no wonder he wished to put off the day of submission. And the poor little girl at Smyrna, waiting there for the young Western prince like the heroine of an Eastern tale! She would give the world to see her photograph; did I think Mr. Pickering would show it to her? But never fear; she would ask nothing indiscreet! Yes, it was a marvellous story, and if she had invented it herself, people would have said it was absurdly improbable." She left her seat and took several turns about the room, smiling to herself, and uttering little German cries of wonderment. Suddenly she stopped before the piano and broke into a little laugh; the next moment she buried her face in the great bouquet of roses. It was time I should go, but I was indisposed to leave her without obtaining some definite assurance that, as far as pity was concerned, she pitied the young girl at Smyrna more than the young man at Homburg.

"Of course you know what I wished in telling you this," I said, rising. "She is evidently a charming creature, and the best thing he can do is to marry her. I wished to interest you in that view of it."

She had taken one of the roses from the vase and was arranging it in the front of her dress. Suddenly, looking up, "Leave it to me, leave it to me!" she cried. "I am interested!" And with her little blue-gemmed hand she tapped her forehead. "I am deeply interested!"

And with this I had to content myself. But more than once the next day I repented of my zeal, and wondered whether a providence with a white rose in her bosom might not turn out a trifle too human. In the evening, at the Kursaal, I looked for Pickering, but he was not visible, and I reflected that my revelation had not as yet, at any rate, seemed to Madame Blumenthal a reason for prescribing a cooling-term to his passion. Very late, as I was turning away, I saw him arrive—with no small satisfaction, for I had determined to let him know immediately in what way I had attempted to serve him. But he straightway passed his arm through my own and led me off towards the gardens. I saw that he was too excited to allow me to speak first.

"I have burnt my ships!" he cried, when we were out of earshot of the crowd. "I have told her everything. I have insisted that it's simple torture for me to wait with this idle view of loving her less. It's well enough for her to ask it, but I feel strong enough now to override her reluctance. I have cast off the millstone from round my neck. I care for nothing, I know nothing, but that I love her with every pulse of my being—and that everything else has been a hideous dream, from which she may wake me into blissful morning with a single word!"

I held him off at arm's-length and looked at him gravely. "You have told her, you mean, of your engagement to Miss Vernor?"

"The whole story! I have given it up—I have thrown it to the winds. I have broken utterly with the past. It may rise in its grave and give me its curse, but it can't frighten me now. I have a right to be happy, I have a right to be free, I have a right not to bury myself alive. It was not *I* who promised—I was not born then. I myself, my soul, my mind, my option—all this is but a month old! Ah," he went on, "if you knew the difference it makes— this having chosen and broken and spoken! I am twice the man I was yesterday! Yesterday I was afraid of her; there was a kind of mocking mystery of knowledge and cleverness about her, which oppressed me in the midst of my love. But now I am afraid of nothing but of being too happy!"

I stood silent, to let him spend his eloquence. But he paused a moment, and took off his hat and fanned himself. "Let me perfectly understand," I said at last. "You have asked Madame Blumenthal to be your wife?"

"The wife of my intelligent choice!"

"And does she consent?"

"She asks three days to decide."

"Call it four! She has known your secret since this morning. I am bound to let you know I told her."

"So much the better!" cried Pickering, without apparent resentment or surprise. "It's not a brilliant offer for such a woman, and in spite of what I have at stake, I feel that it would be brutal to press her."

"What does she say to your breaking your promise?" I asked in a moment.

Pickering was too much in love for false shame. "She tells me that she loves me too much to find courage to condemn me. She agrees with me that I have a right to be happy. I ask no exemption from the common law. What I claim is simply freedom to try to be!"

Of course I was puzzled; it was not in that fashion that I had expected Madame Blumenthal to make use of my information. But the matter now was quite out of my hands, and all I could do was to bid my companion not work himself into a fever over either fortune.

The next day I had a visit from Niedermeyer, on whom, after our talk at the opera, I had left a card. We gossiped a while, and at last he said suddenly, "By the way, I have a sequel to the history of Clorinda. The major is at Homburg!"

"Indeed!" said I. "Since when?"

"These three days."

"And what is he doing?"

"He seems," said Niedermeyer, with a laugh, "to be chiefly occupied in sending flowers to Madame Blumenthal. That is, I went with him the morning of his arrival to choose a nosegay, and nothing would suit him but a small haystack of white roses. I hope it was received."

"I can assure you it was," I cried. "I saw the lady fairly nestling her head in it. But I advise the major not to build upon that. He has a rival."

"Do you mean the soft young man of the other night?"

"Pickering is soft, if you will, but his softness seems to have served him. He has offered her everything, and she has not yet refused it." I had handed my visitor a cigar, and he was puffing it in silence. At last he abruptly asked if I had been introduced to Madame Blumenthal, and, on my affirmative, inquired what I thought of her. "I will not tell you," I said, "or you'll call *me* soft."

He knocked away his ashes, eyeing me askance. "I have noticed your friend about," he said, "and even if you had not told me, I should have known he was in love. After he has left his adored, his face wears for the rest of the day the expression with which he has risen from her feet, and more than once I have felt like touching his elbow, as you would that of a man who has inadvertently come into a drawing-room in his overshoes. You say he has offered our friend everything; but, my dear fellow, he has not everything to offer her. He evidently is as amiable as the morning, but the lady has no taste for daylight."

"I assure you Pickering is a very interesting fellow," I said.

"Ah, there it is! Has he not some story or other? Isn't he an orphan, or a natural child, or consumptive, or contingent heir to great estates? She will read his little story to the end, and close the book very tenderly and smooth down the cover; and then, when he least expects it, she will toss it into the dusty limbo of her other romances. She will let him dangle, but she will let him drop!"

"Upon my word," I cried, with heat, "if she does, she will be a very unprincipled little creature!"

Niedermeyer shrugged his shoulders. "I never said she was a saint!"

Shrewd as I felt Niedermeyer to be, I was not prepared to take his simple word for this event, and in the evening I received a communication which fortified my doubts. It was a note from Pickering, and it ran as follows:—

"My Dear Friend—I have every hope of being happy, but I am to go to Wiesbaden to learn my fate. Madame Blumenthal goes thither this afternoon to spend a few days, and she allows me to accompany her. Give me your good wishes; you shall hear of the result. E. P."

One of the diversions of Homburg for new-comers is to dine in rotation at the different tables d'hôte. It so happened that, a couple of days later, Niedermeyer took pot-luck at my hotel, and secured a seat beside my own. As we took our places I found a letter on my plate, and, as it was postmarked Wiesbaden, I lost no time in opening it. It contained but three lines—

"I am happy—I am accepted—an hour ago. I can hardly believe it's your poor friend E. P."

I placed the note before Niedermeyer; not exactly in triumph, but with the alacrity of all felicitous confutation. He looked at it much longer than was needful to read it, stroking down his beard gravely, and I felt it was not so easy to confute a pupil of the school of Metternich. At last, folding the note and handing it back, "Has your friend mentioned Madame Blumenthal's errand at Wiesbaden?" he asked.

"You look very wise. I give it up!" said I.

"She is gone there to make the major follow her. He went by the next train."

"And has the major, on his side, dropped you a line?"

"He is not a letter-writer."

"Well," said I, pocketing my letter, "with this document in my hand I am bound to reserve my judgment. We will have a bottle of Johannisberg, and drink to the triumph of virtue."

For a whole week more I heard nothing from Pickering—somewhat to my surprise, and, as the days went by, not a little to my discomposure. I had expected that his bliss would continue to overflow in brief bulletins, and his silence was possibly an indication that it had been clouded. At last I wrote to his hotel at Wiesbaden, but received no answer; whereupon, as my next resource, I repaired to his former lodging at Homburg, where I thought it possible he had left property which he would sooner or later send for. There I learned that he had indeed just telegraphed from Cologne for his luggage. To Cologne I immediately despatched a line of inquiry as to his prosperity and the cause of his silence. The next day I received three words in answer—a simple uncommented request that I would come to him. I lost no time, and reached him in the course of a few hours. It was dark when I arrived, and the city was sheeted in a cold autumnal rain. Pickering had stumbled, with an indifference which was itself a symptom of distress, on a certain musty old Mainzerhof, and I found him sitting over a smouldering fire in a vast dingy chamber which looked as if it had grown gray with watching the *ennui* of ten generations of travellers. Looking at him, as he rose on my entrance, I saw that he was in extreme tribulation. He was pale and haggard; his face was five years older. Now, at least, in all conscience, he had tasted of the cup of life! I was anxious to know what had turned it so suddenly to bitterness; but I spared him all importunate curiosity, and let him take his time. I accepted tacitly his tacit confession of distress, and we made for a while a feeble effort to discuss the picturesqueness of Cologne. At last he rose and stood a long time looking into the fire, while I slowly paced the length of the dusky room.

"Well!" he said, as I came back; "I wanted knowledge, and I certainly know something I didn't a month ago." And herewith, calmly and succinctly enough, as if dismay had worn itself out, he related the history of the foregoing days. He touched lightly on details; he evidently never was to gush as freely again as he had done during the prosperity of his suit. He had been accepted one evening, as explicitly as his imagination could desire, and had gone forth in his rapture and roamed about till nearly morning in the gardens of the Conversation-house, taking the stars and the perfumes of the summer night into his confidence. "It is worth it all, almost," he said, "to have been wound up for an hour to that celestial pitch. No man, I am sure, can ever know it but once." The next morning he had repaired to Madame Blumenthal's lodging and had been met, to his amazement, by a naked refusal to see him. He had strode about for a couple of hours—in another mood— and then had returned to the charge. The servant handed him a three-cornered note; it contained these words: "Leave me alone to-day; I will give you ten minutes to-morrow evening." Of the next thirty-six hours he could give no coherent account, but at the appointed time Madame Blumenthal had received him. Almost before she spoke there had come to him a sense of the depth of his folly in supposing he knew her. "One has heard all one's days," he said, "of people removing the mask; it's one of the stock phrases of romance. Well, there she stood with her mask in her hand. Her face," he went on gravely, after a pause—"her face was horrible!" . . . "I give you ten minutes," she had said, pointing to the clock. "Make your scene, tear your hair, brandish your dagger!" And she had sat down and folded her arms. "It's not a joke," she cried, "it's dead earnest; let us have it over. You are dismissed—have you nothing to say?" He had stammered some frantic demand for an explanation; and she had risen and come near him, looking at him from head to feet, very pale, and evidently more excited than she wished him to see. "I have done with you!" she said, with a smile; "you ought to have done with me! It has all been delightful, but there are excellent reasons why it should come to an end." "You have been playing a part, then," he had gasped out; "you never cared for me?" "Yes; till I knew you; till I saw how far you would go. But now the story's finished; we have reached the *dénoûment*. We will close the book and be good friends." "To see how far I would go?" he had repeated. "You led me on, meaning all the while to do *this*!" "I led you on, if you will. I received your visits, in season and out! Sometimes they were very entertaining; sometimes they bored me fearfully. But you were such a very curious case of—what shall I call it?—of sincerity, that I determined to take good and bad together. I wanted to make you commit yourself unmistakably. I should have preferred not to bring you to this place; but that too was necessary. Of course I can't marry you; I can do better. So can you, for that matter; thank your fate for it. You have thought wonders of me for a month, but your good-humour wouldn't last. I am too old and too wise; you are too young and too foolish. It seems to me that I have been very good to you; I have entertained you to the top of your bent, and, except perhaps that I am a little brusque just now, you have nothing to complain of. I would have let you down more gently if I could have taken another month to it; but circumstances have forced my hand. Abuse me, curse me, if you like. I will make every allowance!" Pickering listened to all this intently enough to perceive that, as if by some sudden natural cataclysm, the ground had broken away at his feet, and that he must recoil. He turned away in dumb amazement. "I don't know how I seemed to be taking it," he said, "but she seemed really to desire—I don't know why—something in the way of reproach and vituperation. But I couldn't, in that way, have uttered a syllable. I was sickened; I wanted to get away into the air—to shake her off and come to my senses. 'Have you nothing, nothing, nothing to say?' she cried, as if she were disappointed, while I stood with my hand on the door. 'Haven't I treated you to talk enough?' I believed I answered. 'You will write to me then, when you get home?' 'I think not,' said I. 'Six months hence, I fancy, you will come and see me!' 'Never!' said I. 'That's a confession of stupidity,' she answered. 'It means that, even on reflection, you will never understand the philosophy of my conduct.' The word 'philosophy' seemed so strange that I verily believe I smiled. 'I have given you all that you gave me,' she went on. 'Your passion was an affair of the head.' 'I only wish you had told me sooner that you considered it so!' I exclaimed. And I went my way. The next day I came down the Rhine. I sat all day on the boat, not knowing where I was going, where to get off. I was in a kind of ague of terror; it seemed to me

                                              EUGENE PICKERING

I had seen something infernal. At last I saw the cathedral towers here looming over the city. They seemed to say something to me, and when the boat stopped, I came ashore. I have been here a week. I have not slept at night—and yet it has been a week of rest!"

It seemed to me that he was in a fair way to recover, and that his own philosophy, if left to take its time, was adequate to the occasion. After his story was once told I referred to his grievance but once—that evening, later, as we were about to separate for the night. "Suffer me to say that there was some truth in *her* account of your relations," I said. "You were using her intellectually, and all the while, without your knowing it, she was using you. It was diamond cut diamond. Her needs were the more superficial, and she got tired of the game first." He frowned and turned uneasily away, but without contradicting me. I waited a few moments, to see if he would remember, before we parted, that he had a claim to make upon me. But he seemed to have forgotten it.

The next day we strolled about the picturesque old city, and of course, before long, went into the cathedral. Pickering said little; he seemed intent upon his own thoughts. He sat down beside a pillar near a chapel, in front of a gorgeous window, and, leaving him to his meditations, I wandered through the church. When I came back I saw he had something to say. But before he had spoken I laid my hand on his shoulder and looked at him with a significant smile. He slowly bent his head and dropped his eyes, with a mixture of assent and humility. I drew forth from where it had lain untouched for a month the letter he had given me to keep, placed it silently on his knee, and left him to deal with it alone.

Half an hour later I returned to the same place, but he had gone, and one of the sacristans, hovering about and seeing me looking for Pickering, said he thought he had left the church. I found him in his gloomy chamber at the inn, pacing slowly up and down. I should doubtless have been at a loss to say just what effect I expected the letter from Smyrna to produce; but his actual aspect surprised me. He was flushed, excited, a trifle irritated.

"Evidently," I said, "you have read your letter."

"It is proper I should tell you what is in it," he answered. "When I gave it to you a month ago, I did my friends injustice."

"You called it a 'summons,' I remember."

"I was a great fool! It's a release!"

"From your engagement?"

"From everything! The letter, of course, is from Mr. Vernor. He desires to let me know at the earliest moment that his daughter, informed for the first time a week before of what had been expected of her, positively refuses to be bound by the contract or to assent to my being bound. She had been given a week to reflect, and had spent it in inconsolable tears. She had resisted every form of persuasion! from compulsion, writes Mr. Vernor, he naturally shrinks. The young lady considers the arrangement 'horrible.' After accepting her duties cut and dried all her life, she pretends at last to have a taste of her own. I confess I am surprised; I had been given to believe that she was stupidly submissive, and would remain so to the end of the chapter. Not a bit of it. She has insisted on my being formally dismissed, and her father intimates that in case of non-compliance she threatens him with an attack of brain fever. Mr. Vernor condoles with me handsomely, and lets me know that the young lady's attitude has been a great shock to his nerves. He adds that he will not aggravate such regret as I may do him the honour to entertain, by any allusions to his daughter's charms and to the magnitude of my loss, and he concludes with the hope that, for the comfort of all concerned, I may already have amused my fancy with other 'views.' He reminds me in a postscript that, in spite of this painful occurrence, the son of his most valued friend will always be a welcome visitor at his house. I am free, he observes; I have my life before me; he recommends an extensive course of travel. Should my wanderings lead me to the East, he hopes that no false embarrassment will deter me from presenting myself at Smyrna. He can promise me at least a friendly reception. It's a very polite letter."

Polite as the letter was, Pickering seemed to find no great exhilaration in having this famous burden so handsomely lifted from his spirit. He began to brood over his liberation in a manner which you might have deemed proper to a renewed sense of bondage. "Bad news," he had called his letter originally; and yet, now that its contents proved to be in flat contradiction to his foreboding, there was no impulsive voice to reverse the formula and declare the news was good. The wings of impulse in the poor fellow had of late been terribly clipped. It was an obvious reflection, of course, that if he had not been so stiffly certain of the matter a month before, and had gone through the form of breaking Mr. Vernor's seal, he might have escaped the purgatory of Madame Blumenthal's sub-acid blandishments. But I left him to moralise in private; I had no desire, as the phrase is, to rub it in. My thoughts, moreover, were following another train; I was saying to myself that if to those gentle graces of which her young visage had offered to my fancy the blooming promise, Miss Vernor added in this striking measure the capacity for magnanimous action, the amendment to my friend's career had been less happy than the rough draught. Presently, turning about, I saw him looking at the young lady's photograph. "Of course, now," he said, "I have no right to keep it!" And before I could ask for another glimpse of it, he had thrust it into the fire.

"I am sorry to be saying it just now," I observed after a while, "but I shouldn't wonder if Miss Vernor were a charming creature."

"Go and find out," he answered, gloomily. "The coast is clear. My part is to forget her," he presently added. "It ought not to be hard. But don't you think," he went on suddenly, "that for a poor fellow who asked nothing of fortune but leave to sit down in a quiet corner, it has been rather a cruel pushing about?"

Cruel indeed, I declared, and he certainly had the right to demand a clean page on the book of fate and a fresh start. Mr. Vernor's advice was sound; he should amuse himself with a long journey. If it would be any comfort to him, I would go with him on his way. Pickering assented without enthusiasm; he had the embarrassed look of a man who, having gone to some cost to make a good appearance in a drawing-room, should find the door suddenly slammed in his face. We started on our journey, however, and little by little his enthusiasm returned. He was too capable of enjoying fine things to remain permanently irresponsive, and after a fortnight spent among pictures and monuments and antiquities, I felt that I was seeing him for the first time in his best and healthiest mood. He had had a fever, and then he had had a chill; the pendulum had swung right and left in a manner rather trying to the machine; but now, at last, it was working back to an even, natural beat. He recovered in a measure the generous eloquence with which he had fanned his flame at Homburg, and talked about things with something of the same passionate freshness. One day when I was laid up at the inn at Bruges with a lame foot, he came home and treated me to a rhapsody about a certain meek-faced virgin of Hans Memling, which seemed to me sounder sense than his compliments to Madame Blumenthal. He had his dull days and his sombre moods—hours of irresistible retrospect; but I let them come and go without remonstrance, because I fancied they always left him a trifle more alert and resolute. One evening, however, he sat hanging his head in so doleful a fashion that I took the bull by the horns and told him he had by this time surely paid his debt to penitence, and that he owed it to himself to banish that woman for ever from his thoughts.

He looked up, staring; and then with a deep blush—"That woman?" he said. "I was not thinking of Madame Blumenthal!"

After this I gave another construction to his melancholy. Taking him with his hopes and fears, at the end of six weeks of active observation and keen sensation, Pickering was as fine a fellow as need be. We made our way down to Italy and spent a fortnight at Venice. There something happened which I had been confidently expecting; I had said to myself that it was merely a question of time. We had passed the day at Torcello, and came floating back in

                                    EUGENE PICKERING

the glow of the sunset, with measured oar-strokes. "I am well on the way," Pickering said; "I think I will go!"

We had not spoken for an hour, and I naturally asked him, Where? His answer was delayed by our getting into the Piazzetta. I stepped ashore first and then turned to help him. As he took my hand he met my eyes, consciously, and it came. "To Smyrna!"

A couple of days later he started. I had risked the conjecture that Miss Vernor was a charming creature, and six months afterwards he wrote me that I was right.